First
Comes Spring

ANNE ROCKWELL

HarperCollins*Publishers*

Library of Congress Cataloging-in-Publication Data
Rockwell, Anne F.
  First comes spring.

  Summary: Bear Child notices that the clothes he
wears, the things everyone does at work and play,
and other parts of his world all change with the seasons.
   1. Children's stories, American.   [1. Seasons—
Fiction.   2. Change—Fiction   3. Bears—Fiction]
I. Title.
PZ7.R5943Fi 1985   [E]   84-45331
ISBN 0-694-00106-6
ISBN 0-690-04455-0 (lib. bdg.)
ISBN 0-06-107412-8 (pbk.)

First paperback edition, 1991.

For Hannah,
Elizabeth and Oliver

Wake up, Bear Child.
Look out your window.

The daffodils and tulips are up.
The apple tree has blossoms.

This is what Bear Child wears today—
rubber boots, overalls, a flannel shirt
and a Windbreaker jacket.

For spring has come to town.
Everyone is busy.

What are they doing?

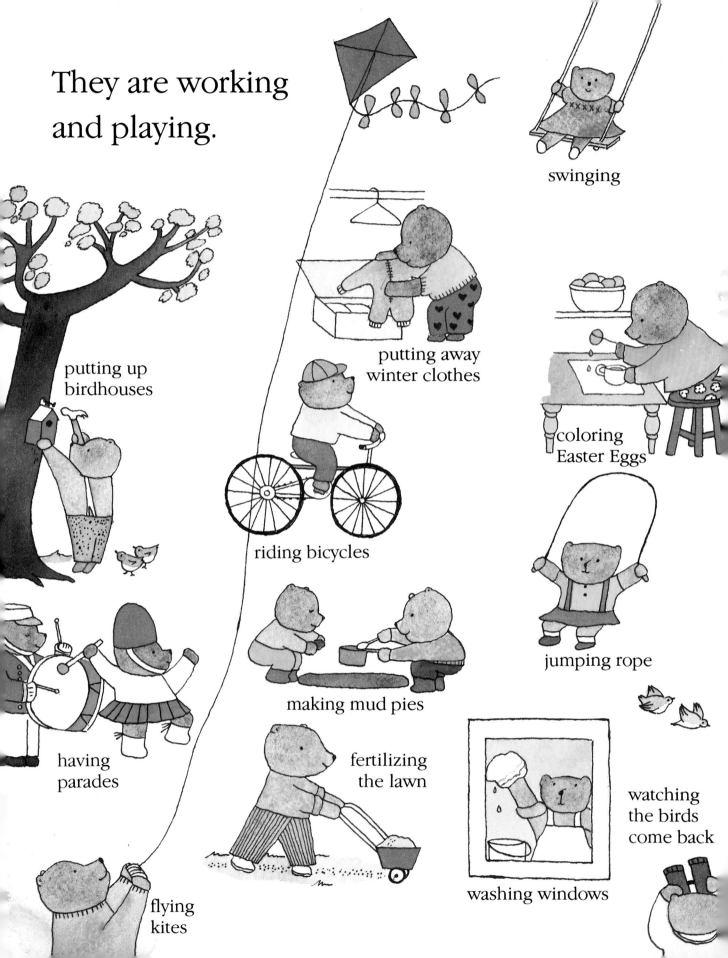

They are working and playing.

swinging

putting up birdhouses

putting away winter clothes

coloring Easter Eggs

riding bicycles

jumping rope

having parades

making mud pies

fertilizing the lawn

watching the birds come back

washing windows

flying kites

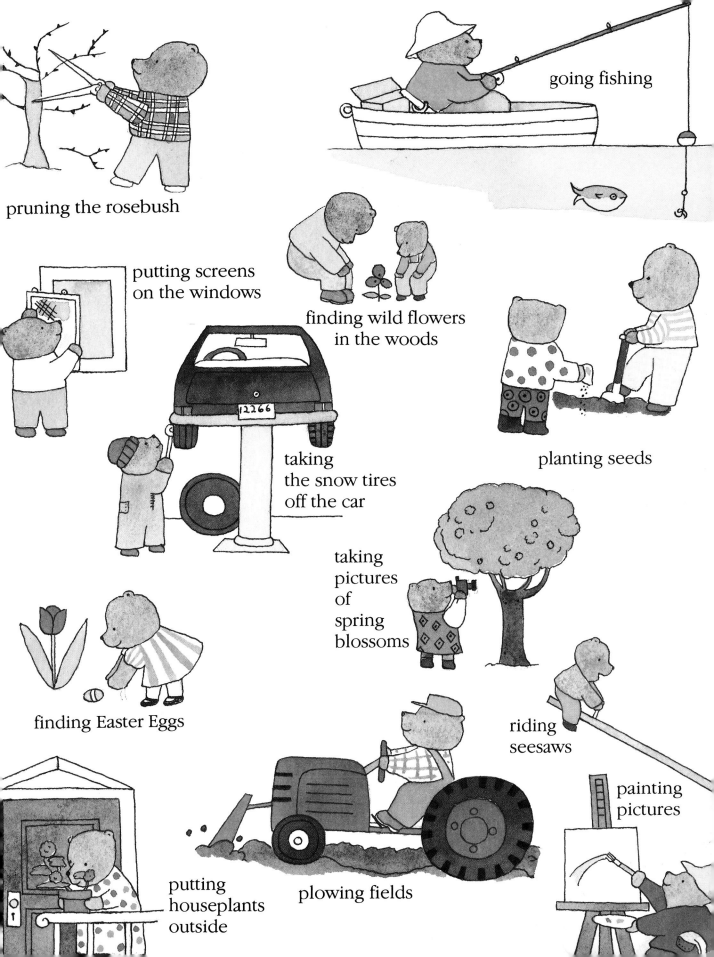

pruning the rosebush

going fishing

putting screens on the windows

finding wild flowers in the woods

planting seeds

taking the snow tires off the car

taking pictures of spring blossoms

finding Easter Eggs

riding seesaws

painting pictures

putting houseplants outside

plowing fields

The grass is green on the lawn.
The apple tree has little green apples.

Now this is what Bear Child wears—
sneakers, shorts and a T-shirt.

For summer has come to town.
Everyone is busy.

What are they doing?

They are working and playing.

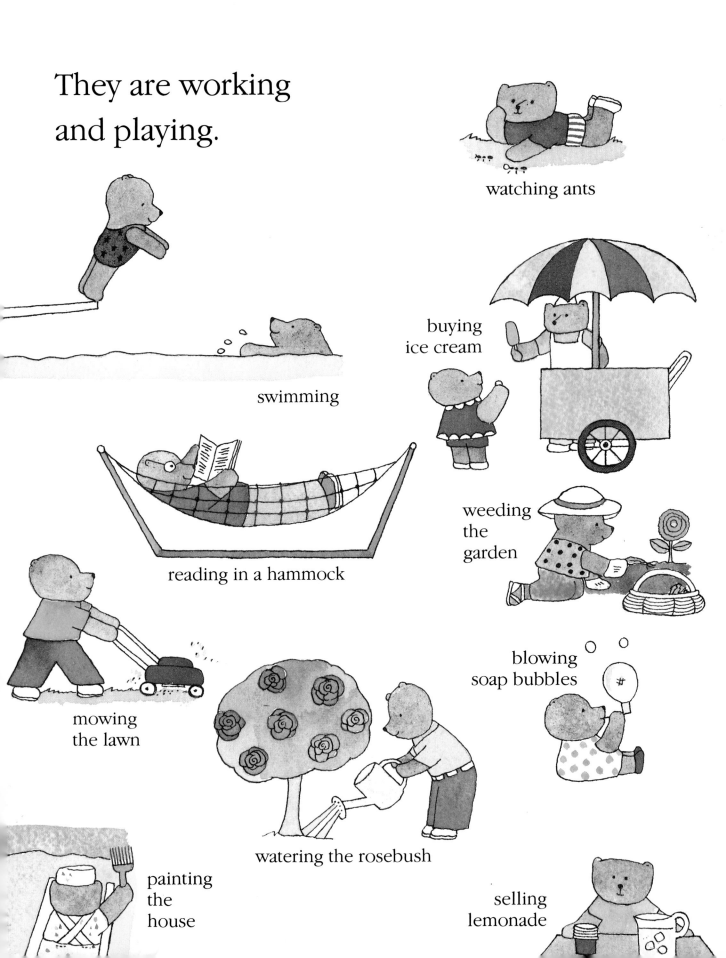

watching ants

buying ice cream

swimming

weeding the garden

reading in a hammock

mowing the lawn

blowing soap bubbles

watering the rosebush

painting the house

selling lemonade

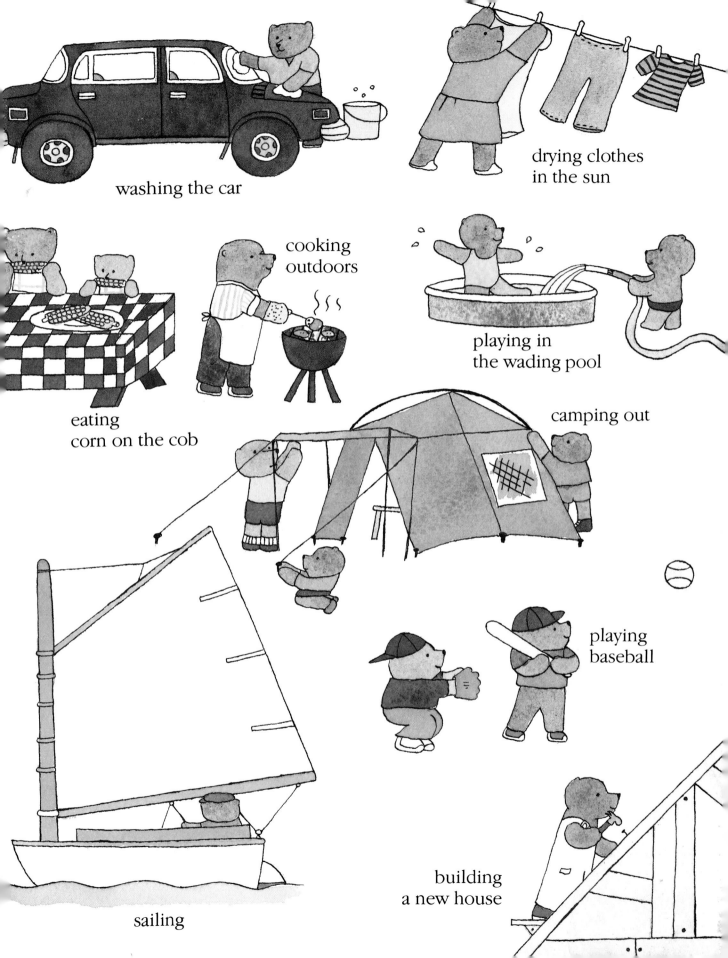

washing the car

drying clothes
in the sun

cooking
outdoors

eating
corn on the cob

playing in
the wading pool

camping out

playing
baseball

sailing

building
a new house

The apples are red.

Orange and yellow leaves fall to the ground.

Now this is what Bear Child wears—
new shoes, corduroy pants, a sweater
and a book bag.

For fall has come to town.
Everyone is busy.

What are they doing?

They are working and playing.

picking apples

watching the birds fly south

canoeing

going to school

building towers of blocks

raking leaves

gathering nuts

playing football

feeding the birds

dressing up for Halloween

carving a jack-o'-lantern

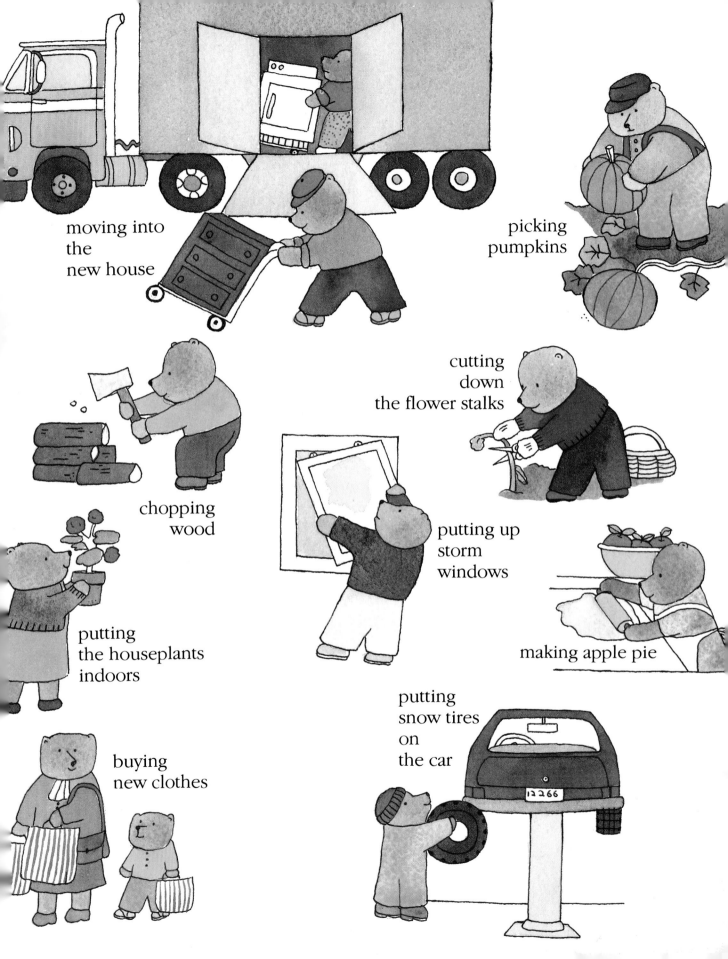

moving into
the
new house

picking
pumpkins

chopping
wood

cutting
down
the flower stalks

putting
the houseplants
indoors

putting up
storm
windows

making apple pie

buying
new clothes

putting
snow tires
on
the car

The trees have lost their leaves.
Snowflakes cover the ground.

Now this is what Bear Child wears—
rubber boots, a snowsuit, a scarf,
a cap and warm mittens.

For winter has come to town.
Everyone is busy.

What are they doing?

They are working and playing.

ice-skating

visiting
Santa Claus

sledding

having colds

buying
presents

lighting
Hanukkah
candles

singing carols

making
angels

drinking cocoa

wrapping presents

plowing the street

putting
a
wreath
on
the door

putting
suet balls
out for
the birds

bringing
a Christmas tree
home

shoveling
the walk

throwing
snowballs

building
an igloo

skiing

putting
lights
on
the
Christmas
tree

baking cookies

The Bear Family sits
by the nice, warm fire.

What will happen when winter
is over?

Spring will come again.